Date: 11/23/22

PA  S0-CRQ-819

LIBRARY SYSTEM

3650 Summit Boulevard
West Palm Beach, FL 33406

FIREFIGHTERS
ON THE SCENE

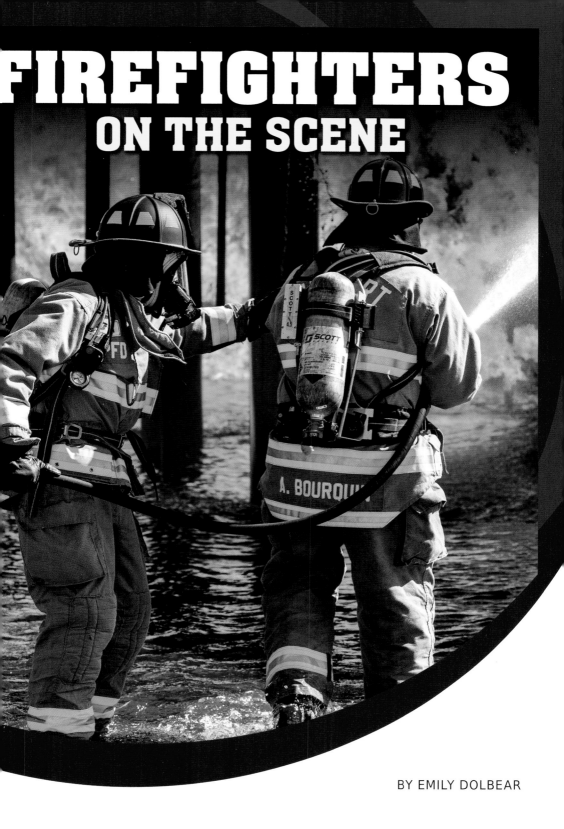

BY EMILY DOLBEAR

Published by The Child's World®
1980 Lookout Drive • Mankato, MN 56003-1705
800-599-READ • www.childsworld.com

Photographs: US Air Force/Wesley Farnsworth, cover, 1; USDA Forest Service/Cecilio Ricardo, 5; US Air Force/Airman 1st Class Nilsa E. Garcia, 6; CatonPhoto/Shutterstock.com, 9; John G. Rusfeldt/Shutterstock.com, 10; Ted Pendergast/Shutterstock.com, 12; sirtravelalot/Shutterstock.com, 14; TFoxFoto/Shutterstock.com, 17; EB Adventure Photography/Shutterstock.com, 18

Copyright © 2022 by The Child's World®
All rights reserved. No part of this book may be reproduced or utilized in any form or by any means without written permission from the publisher.

ISBN 9781503855816 (Reinforced Library Binding)
ISBN 9781503856110 (Portable Document Format)
ISBN 9781503856356 (Online Multi-user eBook)
LCCN: 2021940174

Printed in the United States of America

TABLE OF
CONTENTS

FAST FACTS

What's the Job?

- Firefighters control and put out fires. They protect people and property. Firefighting also helps protect the environment.

- The job requires a driver's license. **Recruits** need at least a high school diploma. Training as an **emergency medical technician** (EMT) is helpful.

- Firefighters have to pass written and physical tests. They must attend a **fire academy**.

- Most firefighters work for local governments. Others work for the state or federal government. Some train specially to fight forest fires. Many work as volunteers.

The Dangers

- Being a firefighter is dangerous work. The job can cause serious injuries and illness.

- Firefighters sometimes die in the line of duty. In the United States, 62 firefighters died at work in 2019. In 2020, there were 96 on-the-job deaths. Thirty-five were due to **COVID-19**.

Important Stats

- There are about 300,000 firefighters in the United States.
- Paid firefighters usually earn about $50,000 a year.
- Through 2029, the need for firefighters will likely grow faster than average.

Chapter 1

A NEW RECRUIT

Catherine Lewis woke up early on March 14, 2021. She dressed in a navy-blue suit and crisp white shirt. Today she would be sworn into duty. She was about to become the first paid woman firefighter in Long Beach, New York.

Catherine was only nine on September 11, 2001. That was the day terrorist attacks brought down New York City's World Trade Center. Like others around the world, Catherine watched it on television. She saw firefighters charging into the burning buildings. They put themselves in danger to help others. Back at school, Catherine kept thinking about their bravery.

Catherine became a teacher after college and graduate school. But she never forgot about those **first responders**. So she took the firefighter exam and got a perfect score. Then she passed the demanding fitness test. At her interview, Catherine talked about what motivated her to work so hard. The next day, she was offered the job.

◀ **A recruit practices handling and carrying equipment. New firefighters need many hours of training to learn the job.**

After the swearing-in ceremony, Catherine took off her COVID-19 mask for a picture. She felt thrilled and nervous. She held up her shiny firefighter badge and smiled. Her first assignment was 18 weeks of advanced training at the fire academy.

Only two days later, Catherine woke up early again. This time, she dressed in an ironed uniform. Catherine headed out, gear bag in hand, for her first day of training.

A dozen recruits sat behind desks at the fire academy in Westchester County. Others joined virtually because of COVID-19. The instructors laid out the schedule. They would cover the skills, knowledge, and fitness needed to serve. A former college basketball player, Catherine felt ready for the physical training. She looked forward to learning more about the chemistry of fire.

But what might have excited Catherine most was the live fire training. That's when the instructors set real buildings on fire for the recruits to put out. They would use hoses and fire extinguishers. Also they would practice opening doors using axes.

Firefighters on September 11, 2001, inspired a young girl. Today, her goal is to be the best firefighter she can be.

Live fire training gives firefighters valuable practice. ▶

Chapter 2

HOUSE FIRE

Fires often start small. Sometimes it is hard to know how they kick off. This time, the first sign was the windows. They were darkened, perhaps by smoke. The fire would have gone unnoticed if a neighbor hadn't called 911.

Four engines were called to the scene of the structure fire. The structure was a wood frame house on a quiet street in Santa Barbara County, California.

Captain Steve Oaks had just started his 24-hour shift. On arrival with his crew, he took a quick trip around the building. The walk around helps establish where victims may be, how to get in and out of the building, and where the fire is. Steve found the windows hot to the touch. There was heat inside but no fire that he could see. No one appeared to be in the house.

◄ **After rushing to the scene, firefighters blast water on a large house fire.**

▲ **A firefighter climbs the truck's ladder to reach the flames shooting through the roof of a house.**

The captain directed his team into action. One firefighter turned off the house's electricity, another turned off the gas. Shutting down the utilities helps keep everyone safe. Other firefighters grabbed a ladder from the truck and hooked up a hose to the hydrant.

Steve's crew suited up and put on their oxygen masks. They had to break open the door to enter. They were able to confirm no one was at home. Setting up a fan helped blow out some of the smoke so they could see and move around easier. But there were no flames to be seen.

Every fire is a mystery to solve. The team got to work. Inside the house, they opened the walls with axes. Up on the roof, they used a chain saw to cut a hole to vent smoke out of the top. No one found any fire.

Finally, a firefighter in the attic located a hot wall. There had to be fire behind it. As her ax broke through the wall, a flame leaped out. Water shot from another firefighter's hose to douse the flame quickly.

Sometimes it's hard to know the source of a fire. Steve wondered if it could have been faulty electrical wiring. Later, investigators would look through the wreckage to find out more.

Steve Oaks and his crew pulled out what they could save from the house. There were some chairs and a sofa that hadn't been damaged. A kind neighbor offered help since the family who owned the home was away on vacation. Then it was back to the station. The crew had to clean up and get ready for the next call.

Chapter 3

NOT EVERY CALL IS A FIRE

Firefighters at Station 12 in Littleton, Colorado, were being called to an MVA. That's short for motor vehicle accident. Justin LaBorde jumped to action. He drew a **fire hood** over his head and stepped into his boots. Then he pulled up his heavy protective pants, held up by large suspenders.

On a run, firefighters often feel a rush of anxiety. Listening to the **dispatcher** on the headset helps focus them. It prepares them for whatever they might face when they climb down from the truck.

As the fire truck pulled up, Justin saw a crumpled car bumper. There was broken glass on the ground. People had gathered on the sidewalk to watch. Two cars had crashed at the intersection.

◀ **Firefighters are first responders. They are trained to respond to many types of emergencies, including car accidents.**

Justin unbuckled his seat belt. He leaped to the ground. It looked like a minor MVA to him. But he knew every accident requires the same attention.

The first responders set to work. They checked if it was safe to enter the accident scene. A firefighter set up cones to guide traffic while Justin assessed each driver. One looked fine as he walked around. The other driver was still in her car.

Justin moved quickly to the woman in the car. Kneeling down, he spoke to her through the car window. She seemed to have no wounds or broken bones. Justin's reassuring words helped calm her. She was able to get out of the crushed car.

After examining the woman, Justin explained she might feel sore for the next few days. A person's neck, back, and knees often ache from the impact of a crash. Justin advised her to see her doctor for follow-up care. He was relieved the accident wasn't more serious.

Not every call that comes in is a fire. Many are other emergencies. Two out of three calls are "medicals."

Firefighters have special tools to help victims ▶ out of their cars after an accident. Firefighters also give first aid to injured people.

Chapter 4

INSIDE THE ALMEDA FIRE

It was a tense time for fire officials in Oregon. The National Weather Service had given the area a red-flag warning. A red flag meant high risk of fire. Temperatures were warm. The air was dry. And the agency was predicting winds up to 50 miles (80 kilometers) per hour.

On September 8, 2020, the chief of Jackson County Fire District Five was on a call with Oregon's fire marshal. The news wasn't good. Oregon fire officials were already working on more than ten large outbreaks around the state. They had no more trucks or workers for additional fires.

Only minutes later, the chief learned of a grass fire in Ashland. It would later be ruled **arson**. Though it was burning in an empty field, the fire bordered the populated Almeda Drive.

◀ **A helicopter drops water on a wildfire. Helicopters and air tankers are often used to help slow a fire's spread.**

In just 15 minutes, six homes on Almeda Drive had caught fire, fueled by the wind. Gusts pushed the flames north. The fire would travel 2 miles (3 km) in the next hour. It would burn right up Pacific Highway.

A second alarm was quickly called. Only about 50 firefighters arrived to manage the growing blaze. Curt Ulrich from Jackson County Fire District Five was one of them. He would soon realize there wasn't enough water or workers.

Curt and the team set up their engines and hoses along Talent Avenue. Their job was to keep the fire from crossing it. They wanted to protect the houses west of the road. But then the hydrants went dry. Even a fire truck carrying 2,000 gallons (7,570 liters) of water made little difference. Every single building seemed to be on fire. And Curt worried about the dangers of breathing the deadly air.

Air tankers overhead, sent by the state forestry service, were one comfort to Curt. Officials on the ground had been communicating by radio with the pilots all day. They dropped red **retardant** from the sky where it was needed. That helped slow the fire's spread.

Still, Curt watched the fire move from house to house, from tree to tree. It was burning through downtown areas, and black smoke was everywhere. The small grass fire had turned into a city fire.

Police officers through their public address systems were ordering people to leave the area. Cars clogged the roads. To the firefighters, it felt like a losing battle. And knowing **climate change** increases the chance of wildfires, they worried about the future.

Finally, the winds changed, pushing the Almeda Fire back onto itself. The fire had traveled more than 14 miles (23 km). It stopped south of Medford, a city of 80,000 people.

In the end, the Almeda Fire destroyed more than 3,000 acres (1,214 hectares). Three people lost their lives. The fire burned down 3,000 structures, including a firehouse in Fire District Five. As deadly and destructive as it was, the Almeda Fire could have been much worse without firefighters like Curt Ulrich.

THINK ABOUT IT

- Would you like to be a firefighter? Why or why not? Which parts of the job appeal to you the most? Which parts don't appeal to you?

- Firefighting requires teamwork. Give examples from each chapter of firefighters working together.

- Why do you think first responders are willing to do such dangerous work?

GLOSSARY

arson (AR-sun): Arson is deliberately setting fire to something. Firefighters can often determine if a fire was caused by arson.

climate change (KLY-mut CHAYNJ): Climate change is long-term changes in the global temperatures and weather patterns. Human actions contribute to climate change.

COVID-19 (KOH-vid nine-TEEN): COVID-19 is short for **co**rona**vi**rus **d**isease 20**19**. It is a potentially deadly virus that is easily spread from person to person.

dispatcher (dis-PATCH-ur): A dispatcher, such as a 911 operator, organizes and sends out the right kind of help in an emergency.

emergency medical technician (ih-MUR-jun-see MED-ih-kul tek-NIH-shun): An emergency medical technician, or EMT, is a person who provides medical care in an emergency. Many firefighters are also EMTs.

fire academy (FIRE uh-KAD-uh-mee): A fire academy is where firefighters go for special training.

fire hood (FIRE HOOD): A fire hood covers a firefighter's head, neck, and face. It protects against intense heat.

first responders (FURST rih-SPAHN-ders): A first responder is someone trained to respond to an emergency, such as a paramedic or firefighter.

recruits (rih-KROOTS): People who have recently joined an organization are called recruits. Firefighter recruits must pass written exams and physical tests during training.

retardant (rih-TAR-dunt): Retardant is a chemical mixture that slows down burning. Air tankers flying overhead can drop retardant on flames to help firefighters gain control of a large fire.

TO LEARN MORE

Books

Bowman, Chris. *Firefighters*. Minnetonka, MN: Bellwether, 2018.

Dittmer, Lori. *Amazing Rescue Vehicles: Fire Trucks*. Mankato, MN: Creative, 2019.

Mahoney, Emily. *What Do Firefighters Do All Day?* New York, NY: Gareth Stevens, 2021.

Websites

Visit our website for links about firefighters: childsworld.com/links

Note to Parents, Teachers, and Librarians: We routinely verify our Web links to make sure they are safe and active sites. So encourage your readers to check them out!

SELECTED BIBLIOGRAPHY

Bernstein, James. "Long Beach Hires First Female Paid Firefighter in Its History." *LI Herald.com*. March 25, 2021. www.liherald.com.

Distenfield, Linda, dir. *On Duty*. Season 2, episode 13, "Escape Route." Aired January 1, 2017, on Amazon Prime Video. www.amazon.com/On-Duty/dp/B079MF68KC.

O'Connor, Erin Patrick. "12 Hours Inside Oregon's Almeda Fire." *Washington Post*. October 20, 2020. www.washington post.com.

South Metro Fire Rescue, Centennial, Colorado. *Firefighter: A Day in the Life*. YouTube. January 16, 2020. www.youtube .com/watch?v=pEIFG7-cmzY.

INDEX

ABOUT THE AUTHOR

Emily Dolbear is the author of many books for young readers. She writes and edits from her home in Brookline, Massachusetts.